The Anagram

EMILIA PAREDES

AuthorHouse™ UK
1663 Liberty Drive
Bloomington, IN 47403 USA
www.authorhouse.co.uk
Phone: 0800 047 8203 (Domestic TFN)
+44 1908 723714 (International)

Published by AuthorHouse 11/28/2019

ISBN: 978-1-7283-9639-2 (sc)
ISBN: 978-1-7283-9638-5 (e)

The Anagram

EMILIA PAREDES

authorHOUSE

On the outskirts of London lived a mysterious 9-year-old girl called Leonie. Leonie loved her name because when people heard it, they said, "Wow! Such a beautiful name!" And when they told her this, she felt so happy that the expression on her face was like a swan's.

At times, Leonie was very quiet, but at others, she was cheerful and sociable, a cute little girl. She had nice curly hair, almond-shaped eyes, and skin the colour of a delicate blend of milk and chocolate.

Leonie was so tall and thin she looked like a figurine. Do you know what I mean?

Leonie's house was near the river of Welsh Harp, a lovely place in London frequented by many people. On occasion, Leonie and her family went to the river to share bread with those who lived there—yes, those who moved in and out of the river, such as ducks, mice, and small animals like those. They would throw bread into the water—looking like happy fools—and when the ducks and geese saw this, they would swim towards the breadcrumbs in single file, looking like a screen saver.

And what can I tell you about the daring mice that roamed the banks of the river? The mice would jump to catch the breadcrumbs before they fell into the water. That was so cute; it seemed like a planned exhibition. Believe me!

One early morning while hurling bread crumbs to the geese that lived in the waters of the Welsh Rivers, Leonie kept hearing a girl's voice, which said to her, "Come, come, Leonie, come!" But Leonie couldn't see the girl anywhere. Drawn to the voice, Leonie went in search of the girl and left behind her family.

Leonie left her parents and went down to the ground in search of the voice called her, where she saw sights that were new to her and heard music coming from somewhere. "I like this place. It is full of beautiful flowers. There are colourful butterflies and bees tasting sweet roses! It is spectacular to see how they dance to this melody. But tell me, why don't you let me see you?" Leonie asked the invisible girl.

"It is better that you just listen to the singing of the birds—to the sound of the river—and enjoy this place. I guess you don't know the mysteries of this river. Come on so that I can show you more," the invisible girl said to Leonie.

"Incredible! It's a small crystal river! It is magical. And who is that beautiful girl? I can only see her back. She has a long white dress, and her hair is as red as a heart," Leonie commented, asking the invisible girl.

Then Leonie tripped on an old log, and while she was falling, she cried out, and her hair became messy. When I saw that, I put my hands over my eyes—what a scare!

Then suddenly, some roller skates arrived onto her feet like magic. The geese, ducks, and mice also kicked on the ice rink over the crystal river. They danced in circles to the beat of the music while the butterflies _with magical wings and amazing colours_ did choreographed movements in the air.

Leonie enjoyed all that was divinely occurring around her. She was living with new friends and did not want any of this to end. Leonie skated without fear from one side of the river to another, opening her arms to imitate the butterflies, leaving the silent wind caressing her face and playing with her curly hair.

"I never imagined living like this! I have so many questions. Tell me what's going on, please," Leonie told the invisible girl.

"What I can tell you, Leonie, is that my story is a little bit sad. You haven't noticed that I am not a happy girl, accompanied but at the same time alone. I just want to ask you if you would mind being my friend. I occasionally come to visit this place," the invisible girl replied.

"I don't think I'd mind being your friend, but I want sincerity. Let me see your face, and after that, we could talk about it," Leonie said, reaching her hand out to the invisible girl, as one does during a serious talk.

A gorgeous horse approached Leonie. It was as white as snow. It had shoes on its hooves and a huge, shining ribbon on its tail as it walked by some poppies.

"Don't be afraid. It won't harm you. Is it not beautiful?" said the invisible girl. "Climb onto the horse, Leonie, and let's gallop near the river. It has a beautiful hidden forest. Let's go on my little horse to infinity.

"Sit here, and I'll tell you my story if you put on this glove and read this book. But first, I'd like to thank you for listening to my voice. I knew you'd come. I called you a lot in the past, but you didn't listen to me at first, because it wasn't time," the invisible girl explained to Leonie, handing her a book and a glove.

"What do you mean *it wasn't time?*" asked Leonie, intrigue.

"putt your gloves on and open the book where for so many years I've been kept, and then I answer your question," ordered to Leonie the invisible girl.

"Many years ago, on a trip from the school where I studied, fellow students and I came to explore this place. It was summer. It was a great day. **_My parents_** and I had lots of fun. I remember that my best friend invited me to go down a road with her, and I grabbed hold of her hand, giving the plan my approval. Then the deeper we went into the forest, the more attractive it became. It was so beautiful that it seemed unreal.

"Not knowing where we were, we saw the air sweep up dry leaves. That cold wind rose so high the leaves went in a spiral. We looked at each other, a little scared and unable to move, and that wind enveloped me and managed to separate our hands. My friend cried out, screaming my name so loud that the waters of the river separated. She told the wind, 'Please don't separate us.' As the wind flew her away, her voice was lost, like waves at sea, like a goodbye without an answer.

"That was the last time I heard it. I have never thought about her for an instant of my life since, and from then until today, I did not see the outside world until now. The whole truth is in that book that you, little intruder, opened. That book tells about a girl whose name contains the letters in the book's title and who would one day come to open it—that is your name Leonie. Your name and my name are like an Anagram, which contains the same letters of your name and my name.

And it tells about the goddess of the river and her red hair, who you saw before to. The book brought me here to the Welsh river to help her. I'm her right hand and her daughter, but I don't know her origin yet. In all our world, she is called the goddess of the river and the Welsh as well, you could see her back because she is half human and half invisible, and you couldn't see me just hear my voice, because I was invisible, now I'm so happy Leonie, because you released me," said Noelia very happy, wearing a beautiful turquoise dress.

"Now, I love the idea of being here with you, but do you?" she asked Leonie.

"Yes, although everything seems to me like a fairy tale. I don't know what to say," Leonie said, a bit dazed. "Is there anything else I do not know?" she queried.

"Have you noticed that I can move your joints—you see, from right to left, right to left? You make me laugh." Noelia was happy and laughed as she directed Leonie's movements.

"Please stop right now, Noelia, and tell me, how can you do that?" Leonie asked, concerned but intrigued.

"As you've put the glove on and opened the book," explained Noelia, "I have been released, and that gives me power to enter your body, but if you don't want that, I can stop. Can I ask a favour of you?" Noelia said with much sadness.

"What now?" replied Leonie.

"I can be by your side and I will do what you ask me, but don't locke me up in the book again, please. I prefer stay here in the real world," Noelia begged Leonie, who played with the horse, while she put her head on her knees with great sadness believing that Leonie ignored her.

"Ha ha ha, OK, move my nose, and move my nose again, please, Noelia. Ha ha ha, please, I think it's so funny. It's like having a double. That sounds weird, but at the same time, it's cool," Leonie explained as she laughed,

7

now entertained by Noelia's power. "All the letters of my name are on the cover of a book, and a girl, who came out of that book, can enter my body. Is this happening to me, or is this all just a crazy dream?" Leonie pointed to her thin body with her delicate fingers.

"No, it is not. It is not a dream. It is as real as the fact that we were both born on Christmas," Noelia insisted.

"Noelia, can I know your world? I mean, can I enter it through the book, because I'm guessing that if you can come out, I could enter as well, yes?" Leonie asked.

"That I cannot deny. I also cannot deny that I am the daughter of the goddess of the Welsh and that is my world. It is extraordinarily enviable— but there is something very valuable that we don't have," Noelia explained somewhat sadly.

"What is missing in your world? Why are you so sad? If you don't want to talk about it, you can throw it in the trunk of your memories—forget it and forgive. But do not cry anymore, Noelia. Come here, and give me a nice hug," Leonie assured her. "Remember that I have eyes also, **and you can wet them like rain to the earth**" Together, they laughed.

Then Noelia told Leonie what saddened her most. "In my world, we don't have freedom, and we don't have that radiant sun, and here, we cannot go beyond the track of ice on the river," she said as she moved Leonie's hair.

"I cannot stop laughing!" Leonie replied, not to Noelia's experience but to her power. "It is funny to know that you're the one who's playing with my two pigtails. I am going to tell you a little secret, Noelia—I'm starting to love you. I don't want to go now. I know that we suffer much when we lose our friends—I know it!"

Noelia stared at her with tenderness and gently held both her hands.

"Oh my God! Where has Leonie gone? Leonie, Leonie!" Leonie's father looked for her around the Welsh Harp river when he and her mother noticed she was nowhere to be seen.

After a morning of searching and calling for her, Leonie's father phoned the police. All the shouts for Leonie went unanswered even when the police intervened.

"Tell me, God, where is my daughter?" Leonie's mother looked desperately at the sky. "Please, God, tell me: Where is she?" The mother cried like the Magdalena.

The family was shattered to hear no news of Leonie.

"This is a moment in which the Word is hidden and one is filled with helplessness," said Leonie's poor father. "I ask myself, indignantly, where is God? Can anyone tell me where God is? How can I look for her without knowing where?" he shouted on his knees.

"Where can that girl be hidden?" the police questioned themselves with their hands on their waists, sweating in fat drops, **while looking for her in the forest, downstream.**

"Oh no! Something just touched my legs. Let's get out of here, folks. Please!" one of the cops—a man—pleaded. I was dying of laughter as he almost pooped in his pants in fear and left.

"This is a serious mission, so stop joking, man," the police chief admonished him.

"It's not a joke. Look as I get goosebumps," explained the poor cop to his superior, setting his eyes like a frightened crab.

Then suddenly, the police spotted Leonie there, along the river. "Look through the trees! There she is. But wait; let's hide. She is talking to someone." The policemen stayed in place, looking to see who she was with, but they didn't see anyone with her. They came out of the trees and found her alone.

"Leonie, what are you doing in this lonely part of the river?" the police chief asked her, taking her in his arms. "Legend says that children who come to this place never come home."

"Leonie, leave that glove. I gather that you wanted to read that book out here, but we have to go," said a police officer. "Little princess, your mother told me that you love books, but that one cannot be opened," he explained to Leonie.

"We will take you home, girl; your family is eager to see you. It has been a long day," said the police chief with a face of relief. He took her in his arms, and they all walked towards the police's car. While the car was moving away, Leonie thought of all she had read and experienced.

"Oh, my little queen! Thank God you are OK!" Leonie's mother shouted, and the family embraced, full of happiness, when the police arrived at the family's house.

"Don't cry, Mommy. I just went to get some flowers for you—just for you," said Leonie, drying her mother's tears while delivering flowers from down the river to her.

Days later, Leonie's mother felt concerned that since the family had moved to London, the girl had locked herself up in her own world created by the books she read. She went to Leonie's doctor, and she asked him about Leonie's behaviour.

"Your daughter is very smart and healthy. Don't worry about that," the doctor explained to Leonie's mother. The girl's parents were uneasy, seeing their daughter so sad since her return from the river.

Another day, they asked Leonie's teacher how their daughter was in his class. "She is one of my best students. She is usually quite calm, and she shares with the others and helps in everything that I ask of them," the teacher commented to Leonie's parents. They felt great relief to know so many interesting things about their little daughter, but they were still not satisfied.

On sunny days, Leonie's parents saw her spending many hours reading, talking alone, and deeply thinking inside the house.

One night, after Leonie's mother kissed her goodnight, Leonie's parents suddenly heard voices coming out of Leonie's bedroom. They ran and hid behind her bedroom door. They were afraid. As they heard their daughter speak, they sat behind the door without making any noise. Then a rumble of thunder made a great sound. Leonie was so entertained that she wasn't afraid of the storm brewing outside.

"I cannot see who's speaking with her," her parents said. Not knowing what to do, they tiptoed out from behind the bedroom door and walked from one end of the house to the other, listening to the storm howling like a wolf.

Meanwhile, Leonie spoke with her invisible friend as if she saw her. "I want to be like my mother says. She tells me that I must have principles. I imagine that when I grow up, I could better understand what she means; now, I think she means that I should think about organizing my things," Leonie explained while dancing with her favourite doll. "Also, she tells me that I have to help others; for that reason, I must start helping at home. I must get an apron and help organize my room, although I don't understand very well those strange things that parents talk about, why she says I should be like that.

"The third thing that she tells me," Leonie added, "is that I must study hard, and I'm worried, because I want to go back to my country, where I have my true friends. Do you understand that?" she queried her invisible friend. "One day, I asked her why we had to move, and she told me, 'To give you a better life.' But I don't have friends here—just you, because you are invisible and you fit in my bag. All my other friends are no longer with me, they are in my Spain, my pretty Spain, where I was born," she said while she wept and dried her giant tears. "What better life? I didn't want to change countries and lose my friends and change my room," Leonie said to her invisible friend, full of sadness.

Then the storm became stronger, and Leonie was afraid and shouted very loudly. Her parents both ran to her.

"I'm here, my little queen," said her father. "Worry never more. Mom and I will always be with you." Her mother caressed her head, and both her parents embraced her with intense sweetness.

"Sleep, my little queen. You must be so tired, even more so than we are," Leonie's mother suggested to her.

"Mommy, read me a story until I fall asleep, please," she begged her mother, who kissed her to comfort her.

"I think you are a little old for that, but I will. You pick one, please," her mother answered. Leonie wished to read her favourite book., called the Anagram.

It had been a tiring day for everyone, so after they read the book, everyone went to sleep at the same time.

"How beautiful it looks, all the view from up here. Of all these beautiful landscapes the Romans enjoyed in their time and today also," said Leonie admired so much beauty. She was marvelled at Rome. She and some new friends she had made at school. They and Leonie's mother had all taken a trip to Rome together.

"Don't make me laugh, Leonie. Are you okay in the head? This is just walls and ruins," said Leonie's friend Emma, pissing off Leonie.

"We are fortunate to see all of this, even in ruins, and corroborate what we have read in history," another visitor told them.

"I love all those goldfish, they are beautiful. I'd like a fish tank, but instead of being here on the Palestinian Hill that is in front of my house," commented Leonie's friend Lisa.

"For the tastes *and* the colours," Leonie said, joking with Lisa. "I'd rather have the Trevi Fountain and Cupid in front my house."

"What is the Trevi Fountain, Leonie?" asked Lisa.

"Nowadays, we have Internet in our life, so I'm going to show you the Trevi Fountain with my little computer," Leonie explained to Lisa. "It's the big fountain where Cupid lives. It's here in the Trevi district in Roma, Italy. One day, I want to see it."

"Really—that's true? I want to see it too. Could you take me with you?" Lisa asked Leonie with the gift of conviction.

"*La Fontana di Trevi* in Italian, or the *Trevi Fountain* in English, is Italy's largest and most famous Baroque fountain. It was constructed by Augustus's son-in-law Agrippa to supply water for the Roman baths," Leonie read to Lisa.

"Seriously, the Internet says that? Why do they say Cupid lives there?" Lisa asked Leonie.

"Here: it says, 'There is no better reason to toss your coin into the Trevi Fountain than just wishing for a return trip to Rome,'" Leonie read to Lisa from off the Internet. "I want to believe in the second legend, which says that if you throw a coin into the Trevi Fountain, you'll find your blue prince. Oh, wow!" Leonie sighed deeply.

"Does that mean you'll have Cupid with you?" Lisa asked Leonie.

Leonie changed the subject when she saw an old cave "We're going to snoop around that cave—Emma, go through the hole. Lisa, go other way—to the door—and I'm going with you, Emma, because I am too scared to go alone," Leonie ordered her friends.

"No, I want to go with you. If the ceiling falls, it'll kill us all together," Lisa claimed, crossing her arms and wrinkling her face.

"That's not the problem, Lisa **you're as fat as an elephant** and will not fit in this hole," Emma said to herself, laughing continuously.

"Be careful Emma, Lisa doesn't hear you, right" Leonie warned.

"Well, this is not my plan. It's the truth. You have to go through the door, Lisa, because this hole is not for an elephant, exactly," Emma replied more loudly, avoiding a laugh.

"Hurry up, hurry up, Lisa. Give me your hand, and I will help you through the hole. Come on, before anyone sees us go into this hole—rather, into all of this here," Leonie said, helping Lisa first get through. "They call it Palatine Hill—they say that the Romans lived here," explained Leonie.

"If it's been over two thousand years since they lived here, we might find their ghosts in here. I want to go. I am so scared. Please, Leonie," said Lisa as she wet her pants.

"I am Remo, and I rip the neck out of anyone that invades my land," one spirit said.

"I am Romolo, and when we join our swords and make a cross, the forces of evil give us power. And there are no forces that rob us of our power," said another.

"Wait, Lisa, we'll find a way out. Don't be afraid, friend," Leonie consoled Lisa while the scare caused by the voices they heard made their hearts all skip a beat.

Then an ice-cold wind invaded the dark hole. The two friends embraced, unable to move. Their teeth made the sound of a violin.

"It's me, Emma. **Have you missed me?**" Leonie and Lisa heard their friend Emma tell them. But they saw her nowhere in sight, which made them even more worried.

"You're dumb, Emma. Why do you behave so badly? It's not right," Leonie claimed to Emma, drying Lisa's tears with her hands.

"Well, it's not the end of the world. We have to go on," said Emma.

"I think you are leaving alone. You are a bad friend, Emma," said Leonie, pretty angry, but in the back of her mind, she wished that Emma would stay with them.

"I am leaving alone, of course," Emma told them.

"Don't worry, Lisa. I am going to take care of you; I promise you," said Leonie.

Suddenly, a great rush of water came through the hole. The water immediately started rising around them.

"We are going to die, Leonie! A lot of water is falling, and we can't get out," Lisa said hoarsely.

"Resist, Lisa. Please, let me find some solution. There must be some way to return," said Leonie, looking to find a light in the dark.

"Oh my God, oh my God—what's going on? Everything is my fault!" Leonie screamed when she saw Emma's lifeless body become buoyant on the water's surface.

"I am going to die, Leonie. Please, fight for your life; you're strong and smart. Don't blame yourself. We all wanted to look around, escaping from our parents. Now, we're suffering the consequences," said Lisa, dying as she struggled in the water.

"Don't leave me, Lisa. I don't know what to do in this narrow, dark, and ugly place," Leonie said, crying.

"Do me a favour, Leonie; tell my parents to forgive me—that I loved them so much," said Lisa, getting as pale as a piece of paper.

"You'll be all right, Lisa. Just think it's a nightmare," cried Leonie.

With her head on Lisa's body, Leonie heard a voice—what she thought was Lisa's spirit's voice—tell her, "I will be here by your side when it is necessary to use your powers and lift your wings like an eagle's."

"You're not moving your mouth to talk; you are now like a spirit. Go rest in peace," Leonie ordered Lisa's spirit, with her heart feeling all scraped up.

"I still can't leave. My duty is to protect you as a friend. Now, you are between a sword and a wall," Lisa's spirit said to Leonie.

"You're right, Lisa. Right now, I am like a boat with no rudder," said Leonie as she struggled to get on top of a rock, watching the torrential waters go through the walls of the dark hole.

Suddenly, Leonie felt a cold air run through her whole body. "You don't see me, but I can see you, Leonie," said Emma's spirit.

"Emma is your name, just in the abstract. But you are not a_god boy, because I saw your dead body. Leave me alone, Emma. I will find the door; now go and rest in peace."

"I have to help you, Leonie. It was me who locked the hole's entry. I know I was a very bad friend. Please forgive me. Now let me help you, Leonie. In a couple of minutes, the torrential waters will cover the hole."

"Don't tell me that, Emma. Then I will die like you and Lisa, and I'll be a spirit also. The saddest thing is Mom and Dad will never see me again," said Leonie, in tears. "Why didn't we see you anymore? Lisa and I were worried about you," Leonie asked Emma's spirit.

"I went to come in the other way, through the door. But when I tried to open the door, a huge rock fell on me," explained Emma's spirit.

"We should never have separated from our parents. We should have understood that we're just children—that we have to obey our parents. There's no cure for all this evil. Look where you are; look where Lisa is. I feel so guilty," said Leonie.

"I don't know what to say," Emma told her.

"We were very rebellious, and now you can see it all," said Leonie.

"Well, everything has its pro and its con, as my dad says. The pro is, now that I am the god boy and I'm a spirit, I can go wherever I want. We can go wherever we want together if I help you," said Emma.

"Sorry, Emma. I can't believe in your help. I feel like you're as bad as you were in life," said Leonie.

"Leonie, look at this. I have my tablet. I am a modern spirit," Emma told her. "Come on; we are here. You can see, in Italy, our parents, the police, the government, and the world—they are looking for us. It's exciting!" Emma showed Leonie.

"Oh, my parents! But I can't believe it; look at how they're crying for me. They love me, and Lisa's parents as well. Don't show me any more. That's not real. I don't know how you invented that!" shouted Leonie with tears in her eyes.

"Now, if I just say a few words" Emma suggested.

"Don't do that. Everything will collapse on top of me," Leonie begged Emma.

"Die like me, Leonie. Now that I have power, I can destroy all of this. I am the god boy. All in this life happens for something. Nothing is coincidental, you know, Leonie," said Emma very angrily. "Well, I think I might do that, because you've never believed in me, and you continue to not believe in me; I am not going to have mercy, Leonie," said Emma.

In response to Emma's threat, Leonie closed her eyes and called on her magical powers, which the voice had told her to use when necessary. "Wings of an eagle, cover my back, and rise to the ceiling."

"But, what are you doing, Leonie?" asked Emma in amazement.

"Lisa, are you? Then it really is just your body lying on these stones. Thank you so much, Lisa, for your help—for something you told me: to lift my wings like an eagle's to defend myself. Even after death, you are a faithful friend," said Leonie with much sadness.

"The water currents will be so strong that they will make a small hole in the cavern and the light will enter. Don't worry about that; the water will drag you where you need to go, and you won't see us again. Don't forget what I asked you to do. Cross your fingers. Bye, dear friend," Lisa's spirit said, watching the waters drag Leonie along.

"Hi. Who are you? It's a little dark, and I can't see you well," Leonie asked, as she could hear someone was close to her. She didn't quite know where she was, how she'd gotten here, or how long it'd been since Lisa's spirit had helped her, but soon, she realized she was on a moving boat.

"Who I am does not matter. What matters is that you are safe in this uncertain world," answered an old man.

"This boat is very rare. The river is beautiful, and the place is great. Look at that; the moon has almost come out," said Leonie, suddenly missing her friends.

"This boat, as you say, is a gondola. You are in Venice. For centuries, this has been people's means of transport; look at the oars," said the old man.

"But where are my friends? It's funny, but I think I've seen you before. On the hill … can it be?" Leonie asked him.

"I don't know. The only thing I can tell you is that I found you at the end of the river, almost lifeless," the old man told her.

"Thanks. I can't remember much—I just know I had some friends," said Leonie, grabbing her head.

"It's not worth it to torture yourself. Life goes on; the present matters—the now. Do not give up," the old man advised her.

"The city is so cute at night—its lights—but where are we going?" Leonie asked him. "Oh no! Mister, what's wrong with you?" Leonie asked the old grey-haired man, as now, in the city lights, she noticed he looked unwell.

"Take the oar. The gondola is sinking. We will perish, my daughter," he said, dying instantly.

What does he mean by calling me daughter? It *w*ondered Leonie as she took the oar and paddled to a dock with all her might.

What can I do now? The grey-haired man told me that the present matters—that if some doors close, others open—and never to give up. The truth of the saying is I have a long way to go, Leonie remembered the old man's words, while walked along the riverbank in her torn dress and bare feet, when the gondola broke.

"Mom! What? You scared me!" said Leonie, jumping out of bed, like a little girl.

"Sorry, daughter. It was not my intention. Open the windows; the sun is already bright and warm," suggested her mother while humming a song.

"You have already done it for me. You're right. Oh, and it's final exams! I lost track of time!" said Leonie, quickly giving her mother a kiss.

"Can you tell me what you wrote, daughter?" asked Leonie's mother.

"It's just a story that a teacher asked me to write—for practice, you know," said Leonie.

"You are already a 20 years old girl. Come here give me a big hug."

"Stop—what you are doing?" Leonie asked her mother.

"I want to introduce you to a friend," Leonie's mother responded, taking her daughter's arm. "Close your eyes," she said, putting her hands on Leonie's face before she said, "Well, now, open your eyes. Leonie, I now introduce you to Sally."

"Pleasure, Leonie. You're as pretty as your mother," said Sally.

"You're not just saying that because she is in front of us, right?" asked Leonie jokingly.

"That could be, it's fun. Your mother is my favourite teacher, and she talks about you all the time. She even has a picture of you on her desk," said Sally.

"Now, I'm like a coconut that didn't fall far from the tree," said Leonie.

"Leonie, the idea is that I am going on vacation to Italy, and I asked your parents to let you come with me," Sally explained to Leonie.

"Don't lie, Sally. Mom asked you to——" said Leonie.

"Yes, yes, Leonie," her mother interrupted and apologized, "I thought it would be a new experience for you. Daughter, it will be a gift from your parents for finishing your classes. You deserve it."

"I don't have the words. I don't know how to thank you for how good you are to me. I love you, but this isn't necessary. Just being by your side is more than enough," Leonie told her mother.

"I'm here, bathed in tears. How touching," said Sally, watching the scene.

"I'm sorry, Sally," Leonie's mother apologized.

"Leonie, realize that we have known each other for a lifetime. We will have a good time. We are going as a group; my friend Emmanuel will be there as well," Sally tried to convince Leonie.

"I'd like to surprise my mother and take her with us too. Do you think she fits into the puzzle?" Leonie asked Sally.

"Of course; she will be a pleasant addition. She can be like our tutor. Leave it to me. I'll take care of her," said Sally mischievously.

"But the trip is for … but …" Leonie's mother babbled when Sally made her the invitation.

One month later, as they embarked on their trip, Leonie told her father, "*Arrivederci*, Daddy."

"Poor guy; we could have invited him too. It doesn't hurt you to leave him?" Sally asked Leonie.

"No, because I plan to give them a second honeymoon one day. Plus, he has a business trip and can't come. It's also my mom's dream to go," replied Leonie.

"If only <u>Sally</u> knew that he is not my true father," said Leonie then whispered to herself.

"Did you say something, Leonie?" asked Sally.

When they finally arrived in Italy, Leonie's mother, impressed, shouted, "No, no, no, a pinch, please. I'm dreaming. Wow, wow, wow!"

"It's your girlhood dream fulfilled. Mom, I'm so happy for you," said Leonie.

"I wasn't expecting so much, daughter—having you grow up and make my dream come true. I never told you about my dream," said Leonie's mother.

"A little bird told me, so enjoy it. Look, Sally and I have prepared a tour. We can go to the Roman Coliseum first," Leonie explained to her mother.

On their tour, Leonie's mother said in wonder, "How interesting it is to be in the Roman Coliseum, as I have read about it."

Later, while resting under an olive tree in the gardens of the Roman Palatine Hill, Sally joked, "In this tremendous sun, we are toast, fresh out of the oven, ready to eat."

"You can't catch me," Leonie played with her mother.

"Why don't you grab me? La la la la la," **said** her mother, following her game.

"You look like two girls playing hide-and-seek," Emmanuel said to Leonie and her mother.

"That's a good idea. Let's all play behind the walls of the Palatine Hill. It's awesome to see that they still exist in real life," commented Sally.

"That is not for me. It is a lot of walking, and my age does not help me," said Leonie's mother.

"Don't say that, Mom. You're strong like an oak tree. Look, we're young, and we're tired too," said Leonie.

"Well, our next stop is Pisa, the tower that bends but does not break!" Sally shouted, jumping.

"Here—we can take a bus, and then we get off there," said Emmanuel, leading the group.

"Are you having fun, Mom? I hope you are having a great time," Leonie asked her mother, kissing and hugging her.

"I am as happy as an earthworm. I am like water on high, as the flow rate carries clean water. Thanks, daughter. You are the sun," her mother replied excitedly.

"Wow that's the Pisa tower; I am in Italy. I still feel like I'm reading a book from my rocking chair on the terrace of my home," Leonie's mother said, watching the tower live and in person when they'd reached their second destination.

"Laugh; don't cry. Just enjoy the values, the opportunities that life gives you," their small group sang to Leonie's mother.

"Next, we will make our triumphant entrance in Venice," said Emmanuel.

When they arrived in the city, Sally shouted, "Ladies and gentlemen, we have come to the floating city, which is … which is Venice!"

"Oh my God! Oh my God, this is really a dream. Now, I feel like I am reading a travel magazine. It gives me something …" With that, Leonie's mother passed out.

"Mom, Mom, wake up! Look at the beauty, Mom." Leonie tried to wake her mother by fanning her with her hands. Sally managed to wake her by picking up a nearby bucket, filling it with water from the canal, and emptying it on top of her.

"So it is not a dream. Come on, guys. Let's take our bags and leave them at the hotel and go explore Venice," said Leonie's mother after that good, wet wake-up Sally had given her.

"Let's eat at that restaurant in front of my nose. They say it's the best in Venice," Emmanuel suggested. "I hope it is."

"For me, a coffee without sugar. __But my husband changed me,__" joked Leonie's mother. "My husband taught me that sugar shortens life."

"We will be going to a spooky costume party tonight, so I suggest that after lunch, we go buy our dark clothes," Emmanuel said, changing the subject.

"Boy, you talk about it like it will be a funeral instead of a party. Don't be afraid, darling. Emmanuel is exaggerating; believe me," Sally said, reassuring Leonie's mother.

Later, while they were all out shopping for costumes, Emmanuel jokingly asked Sally, "Tell me, how is this pink wig in combination with my skirt?"

"I was afraid you were gay. Now, I have no doubt. Your feet smell horrible, Emmanuel," Sally replied.

"You're a heavy person and very envious as well," Emmanuel said to Sally.

"We should get dressed like Roman women in olden times," Leonie suggested to her mother.

"I don't really like those costume parties; there're not for me," she replied.

"Mom, you will have a costume on, and nobody will recognize you. There will be people from all over Venice there. It will be a dynamic party, I'm sure," Leonie said to her mother, trying to talk about it in a convincing way.

"No, I would prefer to go see the city at night, take pictures, and walk along the shore of the port. It must be spectacular, like in magazines, in documentaries, and even on YouTube—they all show some dream photos," Leonie's mother told her.

Leonie thought about what her mother was saying and asked her, "How is this dress?" dancing and imagining she was hearing music by Mozart.

"You look like an angel. You'll be the most beautiful of the party."

"I'm not sure you should be out alone at night in Venice, Mom," Leonie finally told her mother.

"Don't worry about me; I'll be fine. I know this place as if I've been here before," Leonie's mother replied.

"Give me a strong hug—very strong, Mom. I love you to the end of the universe and back," Leonie said.

"My little princess, you go to the party. In the meantime, I'm going to take some pictures, OK? And we'll all have a great time."

"Day and night, Venice is nice," said Sally, thinking about the costume party.

Later, while Leonie's mother was still out exploring Venice, she placed a video call to her husband back home. "Love, I called you so you can see where I am. Look here," she said, showing him her view from a bridge. As soon as she did so, she realized that something terrible must have just occurred, because she was hearing incredibly loud noises moving through the city.

"What's all that noise? I hear the sound of police cars, love. Are you OK? Where are you?" Leonie's father asked his wife, worried.

"I'm here in Venice, love. It seems to me that something serious has happened in the city, and there is a lot of movement in the small Venetian streets."

"Love, go back to the hotel. I understand that there is a lot of security in Venice, but it is not good to be on that bridge alone. Call me when you are there. I love you," said Leonie's father.

"Love, check all the television news; check the news on the Internet and your mobile ..." Leonie's mother said, crying with a dry throat.

"Everyone was dressed in black: it was a party of black costumes. Nobody was saved in that place. And since then, her mother has been bedridden. She does not speak, just swallows food through tubes. Leonie's absence and that cruel death have destroyed our lives," Leonie's father informed a television reporter., one year after the event.

"It is said that disguised demons entered that place and sucked the blood out of all those people, leaving them as dry as leaves. Do you believe it?" the reporter asked Leonie's father.

"I don't know what to believe. Leave me alone with my love. I want to immerse myself in her pain, wipe away her tears," Leonie's father said with immense sadness, kneeling at the feet of his love—his wife.

Printed in the United States
By Bookmasters